insomnia and the aunt

insomnia and the aunt
tan lin

CHICAGO: KENNING EDITIONS, 2011

COVER DESIGN BY CRISIS STUDIO
INTERIOR COMPOSITION BY PH. DIO

PUBLISHED IN CHICAGO BY KENNING EDITIONS
KENNINGEDITIONS.COM

3RD PRINTING, SPRING 2023

DISTRIBUTED TO INDIVIDUALS AND THE TRADE BY SMALL
PRESS DISTRIBUTION, 1341 SEVENTH STREET, BERKELEY,
CA 94710-1409 1-800-869-7553 / SPDBOOKS.ORG

for my mother and father
who arrived "here"

On March 10, I board a plane to Seattle, rent a white Honda Acura and drive eighty-seven miles to Concrete, Washington and the Bear Park Motel, a cheap motel on the western edge of North Cascades National Park that is run by a half-Chinese, half-English woman who happens to be my aunt. My aunt once told me that the rooms in the motel have seven foot ceilings and are lined with cinderblocks painted yellow. I have a few old photographs of this motel, most of which were sent to my mother, who thinks a motel in the middle of nowhere is some kind of crime against nature and has never visited, even though my aunt has extended numerous invitations on post cards. On the day before I leave, I show my mother a postcard of the motel and a photo of a woman in a cowboy hat. My mother glances at both and says, "I do not remember."

From a genealogical perspective, my aunt and uncle started their lives in America with a Chinese restaurant in Spokane and later in Seattle. Their first restaurant went out of business, they moved to Seattle to open another one, I think it was called Ming's Garden, but they got tired of serving people American Chinese food, so in the early 80s they decided to close the restaurant down and travel east, *into* the wilderness. They settled in a place near North Cascades National Park, near an Indian reservation. My aunt has always told me, in an inconsequential sort of grammatical inversion, that this is "the story of your lives" only backwards, from America to the real America, from China to somewhere you've never been before. And like most Orientals in the mid-seventies (or "Asian people" as they have been called since the mid-nineties), there was never the slightest bit of emotion on her face when she told me this story. Someone said "The Oriental, we are good at killing emotions," and I think that person was right.

The drive from Seattle to Concrete takes me an hour and fifty minutes. It is late afternoon when I arrive. I pull into the spot in front of the lobby window and pull

459:—LAKE WASHINGTON PONTOON BRIDGE, SEATTLE, WASHINGTON

ONLY CONCRETE PONTOON BRIDGE IN THE WORLD.   47647

my bags from the trunk. My aunt is crying in front of the lobby window, which is back lit like a movie set. She runs out, yanks the duffel from my hands and bump drags it two or three steps in front of me to room seventeen, which is the room my aunt always takes me to whenever I visit, just as Salvador Dali when he came to New York always stayed at the St. Regis and always in room 1628. Whenever I visit during the next decade, my aunt will perform the same actions, with the same deliberate energy I associate with following a recipe one knows very well or watching re-runs on TV. She will cry in exactly the same manner, in front of the neon NO VACANCY sign in the window, with the same uncontrollable wailing and tears and half-Chinese words I do not understand. None of this I can hear very well through the glass. When I think of these actions, they give off, like the paradox surrounding a guess, the appearance of slightness inside moments that have already happened, as if my aunt's life were endlessly re-passing a single point in time, like an actor in a sitcom or a car going past the same highway exit night after night on its way home. And yet the repetition of my aunt's tears meant something completely different ten years after it first happened.

I don't remember much of this motel, but there is, as I gather from the post cards and photographs, an occasional painting in the rooms and once, when I first thought about visiting my aunt, when I was in high school, I remember seeing a photograph of a door that had been kicked in and which my aunt had pasted onto the back office wall. I don't know if this memory is based on something my aunt wrote me in a letter or said to me or whether I clipped the picture from a magazine many years later. The only photograph of my aunt that I have managed to hold onto through the years has her wearing a white cowboy hat and dark sunglasses that seem out of place in the wilderness, and that signal the sort of disruption or lie that I associate with Asians in the movies or in Ohio where I grew up, or Asians in fast food restaurants like McDonalds, where I have never eaten and where I have never seen a Chinese person eating. I have watched hundreds of movies with Asians and fake Asians in them, and the one thing that makes them all the same (except the white Asians) is that the Asians never stare into your eyes through the glass of a TV screen and you are never allowed to look too deeply into theirs. I think it is for this reason that whenever I think about my aunt, and TV for that matter, I can never remember my aunt's eyes (they appear to belong to someone else), and think instead of Robert Redford, who said in an interview that it is necessary for the body to lie to the mind (not the other way around) when acting and that the various strata of lying are continually searching for each other in the wilderness that most people call the truth and that my aunt calls television. For my aunt, TV can never really lie because it is on all the time, unlike the theatre, where there are all sorts of changes of scenery and which as a result goes on and off and is thus the perfect medium for telling lies one after another. But in my aunt's motel, the TV never goes off and all these changes are not changes at all; they're commercials.

For my aunt, and I think for Robert Redford, lying was a specific thing, like a baby crying in a room or an animal with a soul or, at the least, those mental states that scientists believe trigger particular actions like chasing after a bug or moving to another branch, which is to say that lying is the most sincere way of expressing oneself, and the best way anyone has of connecting one thing to another. As Paul Newman said, lying is a highly flirtatious and mechanical form that the body has of creating a gene pool. For this reason lying is never natural (in the reproductive sense)[1] and is best expressed with the eyes, whose motions

1 How to Detect Lies - body language, reactions, speech   patterns

The following techniques to telling if someone is **lying** are often used by police and security experts. ... The guilty person may speak more than **natural**, adding unnecessary details to convince ... Related Books: **Never** be Lied to Again ...

www.blifaloo.com/info/lies.php - Cached - Similar

WELCOME TO YAKIMA, WASH.
THE EASTERN GATEWAY TO MT. RAINIER

are perceived to be distinct from the somaform and somatic expressions. Everyone thinks you can make love with your eyes but really the only thing you can do with your eyes is lie with them. People who cry a lot tend to have more affairs than those who don't. Lying and having sex are best done with the eyes completely closed. To lie and have sex at the same time is one of the greatest things anyone can do. It is of course much harder to lie when staring directly at someone or something (like food) that one likes. It is impossible to lie to a computer that's turned off. A blank computer screen can still remind us of a face.

In the years since my aunt's death, I have often thought about what holds the parts of a family together, and I think it may be lies told in families almost like ours, or, in other words, American families in Ohio, not Chinese ones in Seattle. When we were growing up, my Chinese parents never told me much about my half-Chinese aunt, whether she was an aunt on my mother's or my father's side, whether she was a real aunt or just a Chinese auntie, or whether she was an American person who looked half Asian. I called her *kan-ma*. I am pretty sure *kan ma* means person related to a mother, even though *nai nai* and *wai po* are the words for grandmother on the father and mother's side respectively, and she was neither one of these. I think *kan* means *dry*, and so *kan ma* is probably a *dry mother* or one who doesn't nurse you. I never called her *a yi*, who I think was a real aunt on my mother's side and lived in New Jersey even though she was twenty years younger than my mother and a step-sister to her. My step-aunt's Chinese name was probably not quite actually hers, and likewise, my aunt's name is not quite right either. My mother called my aunt "Big Sister," and sometimes "Second Sister," none of which made much sense, as my mother has told my sister and me that she only had one sister, a half-sister, who was the daughter of her father and a second wife. Some names are simply too complicated or literal for American English, like a mother with no milk or an aunt who is not an aunt but is called one anyway. At any rate, when thinking of my aunt, I think of her at odd hours of the day or evening, like a television playing accidentally in another room, just as I think of my mother and father giving themselves American names when they arrived in Seattle. The names for my family are linked, like a mirror or perhaps a footnote, to the physical world and to social inconsistencies and historical accidents. In other words, my mother and father rarely saw my aunt in my presence, except maybe once on our first and only family visit to a Chinese restaurant in Spokane. Some relatives are meant to be imagined years before or after they died.

After my aunt checks in the last of the guests, I go see her in the front office. She rustles through the desk drawers and pulls out one can of Franco-American SpaghettiO's, one can of Chef Boyardee, two plastic bowls, a few plastic forks and a moist towelette. A white Toyota Camry and a grey Subaru are parked, tail in, towards the lobby window, just beyond the NO VACANCY sign. My aunt empties a can into an aluminum pot. What looks like a mom, dad, and two kids are pulling duffel bags and canoe paddles from a roof rack. Two kids are unloading the white car.

"The white one? " I ask.

"Teenagers."

"How old?"

My aunt shrugs. "Their license is almost expired. Ohio. Maybe as old as you."

I try to do the math in my aunt's English. "Car or them?"

My aunt shrugs. I recognize the shrug of someone who has been lied to.

"The Toyota?"

"A family called Bumas." My aunt switches channels and drops the remote in her lap. She points to something outside like something on TV.

"You mean the hatchback?"

"People from Queens."

My aunt, forgetting we are watching TV in America says, "*Hah. ge dong, si teou lie tyan. shia lie,*" instead of "*Nyyg dong. shi diaw de dih. shiah le,*" using the Paoting dialect she learned from her nanny when she was (Chinese) age seven, and which I do not speak.

I translate the words aloud, "That... thing... has... dropped.... to... the.... floor?" My aunt nods.

I nod back. The sun is setting. My aunt remembers more details, in Jewish English. "Shaskan. A dad. They have a tent and a wok. Rhoda."

"Who?" I squint into the window. "They look pale."

"They must be real," my aunt says, "with a name like that."

"Where are they going?" I ask.

"Camping," my aunt says. The taller boy drops a blue and white plastic cooler that has "Playmate" written on it. It hits the pavement and bounces against the Subaru. The Camry girl smiles. I hear Coke cans rolling under a car.

"Did they ask about bears?"

"No, they asked about TV."

My aunt and I laugh a little. This sort of conversation goes on while dinner heats up, with me wanting to know more about the most recent arrivals and my aunt wanting to watch more TV. A motel in the middle of nowhere is kind of a distracted family, and my aunt and my TV watching is pretty much an unchanging changing seasonal routine whenever I visit, eating and chatting slowly and occasionally as the night wears on, with the routine broken up only when the late night news comes on at three or four a.m. and my aunt shuffles in her Chinese slippers to the vending machines in the lobby where she buys some Ho Hos and puts them in a freezer for our dessert.

My aunt hands me a bowl of Chef Boyardee and we settle in, in front of the TV. On top of it, she has arranged a few Garfields, a Lucite pen holder, vanilla incense, and a memo pad from an auto glass shop in Concrete. The pen holder and the memo pad are taped to the TV. Because there are only one or two channels that we get and they frequently fade out or cloud over with interference, most of our TV watching is involuntary and achronological, a kind of anthropological dumb show wherein we watch segments of competing old westerns, switching to late night shows and Jackie Gleason re-runs when reception is particularly atrocious. My aunt lights the incense and turns on a show about African game animals. On a show that is probably Mutual of Omaha's *Wild Kingdom*, we see a female lion placidly sitting in the grass with a young gazelle's neck in its mouth.

My aunt looks up. "What is a three-legged thing for sitting?" I look away from the TV. "Do you want a Ho Ho?" my aunt adds.

"Ho Hos after dinner," I remind my aunt.

"How many letters?"

"Five," my aunt says in Chinese.

"Stool," I say.

We watch the gazelle. Its breathing is rapid and shallow. Its eyes are glassy. The gazelle is seven months old and does not have its legs yet. The narrator says it is in shock brought on by the pressure of the lion's powerful jaws and the weight of its body. My aunt stares at something on top of the TV. "I can see the gazelle's eyes."

"When will the gazelle die?" I ask my aunt.

"Already dead."

My aunt has trouble understanding when something is dying on TV and when something is dead in real life and that *already dead* is not the same thing as the fiction of watching it on TV. "They won't show that on TV."

"Gazelle. Already dead," my aunt says. She adds, "not already dying."

The show ends with an African sunset. Before the credits roll, my aunt turns to a show about men pulling tractors with their teeth.

Because we don't watch TV continuously or closely, a few seasons or even decades of TV can pass before us without us quite realizing it, and by three or four a.m. my aunt seems to be a part of the anthropology of somebody else's TV set. And yet watching my aunt watch TV makes me believe something about myself, like I am going to walk into a room and say something to someone who is there, like what are we having for dinner tonight? or did you hear about the person who put a quarter in someone else's parking meter and was arrested for it? or it makes me want to talk about my family sitting around the TV listening to Chet Huntley talk about the Vietnam War when my mother says it is time to get up and eat dinner and we get up and eat our rice with red chopsticks out of bowls (one of them is green) my father made and sometimes we never say anything at dinner. Watching my aunt watch TV is deeply optimistic and romantic because most of these things I am thinking about never happen when I am alone, but they remain a kind of background music of "splendid conversation" (Emerson said that about Carlyle's writing once) and everyday things going on in my head. For the two of us, watching television slowly, as evening goes into morning and the sound going in and out, is a lot like watching a plant reproduce.

Although we're vague in what we watch, we have communal watching preferences. [2] We especially like to see things about sharks, any form of mental illness, physiological studies of sex in humans (as if they were primates), dating shows of people my age or just a little bit older, strange

2 Age | audiencescapes

This could signify a more **communal watching** approach to television. For those 25 and older, the difference was not as large (19 percent of those 25-44 had ...

www.audiencescapes.org/country-profiles/uganda/.../age-228 - Cached sporting events—like women spitting kidney beans into tin cups—and commercials during peak broadcast moments. These are all extremely soothing to my aunt and me. We also appreciate stock car races and occasionally college basketball—with their interesting kinesis of movement and seeing whose flickering reminds me of kissing or stir fry. For my aunt, live TV of any sorts, except for the late night talk shows, is an unwatchable void. For her, TV is not a screen upon which remote images flicker or a metaphysical conduit for the selling of soap but furniture that moves like a glacier through American life, picking up all sorts of magnetized debris and junk which it affixes to the other side of the TV glass, like the rear view mirror in a pick up truck that reflects things passing by.

The tractor pull ends. My aunt switches to channel five. "No luck," she says.

Sometimes we get four or three but tonight it's channel five. A man in a black suit waves a baton in front of an orchestra pit. People lounge on a lawn, drinking from real wine glasses balanced on blankets.

"Ugh," I tell my aunt. "It's the Boston Pops. It's probably live." My aunt dislikes live broadcasts of operas or concerts. Such things feel canned to my aunt, as if they have been rehearsed once in real life and once on television, or, in other words, once in somebody else's life and once in ours. White noise comes from under the sound of the instruments. My aunt, forgetting that she holds the remote, tells me to switch, then switches. The screen comes into focus. Kids rush into a kitchen. Their clothes are covered in mud and grape juice. The mother frowns and smiles. "I like this," my aunt says. She looks at me, "we use Tide."

For an immigrant like my aunt, America is not the images on a TV, it basically is the TV, which is why she decorates it with paper doilies, vanilla incense sticks and stuffed Garfields. This is also why my aunt thinks all TV, even live TV, is canned, and why she thinks America is basically not a place or even an image, but furniture. For my aunt, the live broadcast of the Vietnam War of my youth and her early middle ages resembled a re-run. My aunt accordingly has very few memories of violence or even racism in America. TV has made her forget all these things. Likewise, it is very hard for me to remember her even though I miss her intensely. The more I miss her the more she becomes furniture or a TV commercial for Tide detergent.

Anyway, my aunt thinks TV should be a relaxing, circular consumer activity that is continually on, and basically I think there is no need for it to pretend to do something it does not do very well. No TV I know is capable of ideological domination although it might be capable of clairvoyance or bringing back the dead. So while we are watching late at night, the Sylvania sits unambiguously on her desk. It puts our world to sleep when nothing much is happening, and in that way it gives the world back to us second-hand, in the only way we know how to understand it. If live TV is disturbingly real, canned TV for my aunt is a function of reincarnation, or maybe morphology, at once vague, causal and novelistic. I think it makes loneliness tangential to that process in which becoming American is unloaded to advertisers, and everything is furnished within this medium of exchange. I know this because in the end everyone walks out of the room and turns off the TV without doing anything and because a family like ours is very hard to imagine without a TV playing somewhere in the background.

Hands down, my aunt's favorite person late at night is Conan O'Brien, whose stiffness before the camera and guests and inability to tell a joke at the right speed or ask an interesting question and then *actually wait* for the answer is endlessly enlightening, because it is not so easy to make talking sound as if it were already a re-run or a joke whose punch line had come and gone before you had a chance to catch it. Bad interviewing skills have made Conan an onscreen relative for my aunt, and maybe even an image of her marriage to Uncle Bing. At any rate, Conan O'Brien is the only person on TV who can make my aunt understand that no joke is very funny, especially to family members who don't get it. This is usually done by Conan *repeating verbatim* things that *were just said* by one of his guests and then laughing right after he has said it, and everyone who is watching knows this is not funny. It is nerve wracking to hear oneself repeated just as that other person starts to laugh. Laughing that is delayed makes my aunt and me feel a little stupid and then a little relieved that someone is laughing for us.

My aunt did not completely understand why someone else was laughing for her late at night with me, and because of this, the time for her laughter has never really quite arrived at the moment I think it has. I think you really love what people can't do inside themselves, even if the things are dumb. Laughter after all, like crying, is a kind of communal family chore, which is why the networks invented laugh tracks and why in certain countries you hire mourners to come to a funeral and weep for you. Less distant relatives like my aunt are usually too grief stricken to grieve in the present, which is why most grieving takes place long before or many years after someone has died. Having someone else laugh on TV for my aunt was the most relaxing of things because it allowed someone else to have her feelings while she was watching. TV, and I think all TV is great, is not about having emotions but escaping from your least predictable emotions. Of course, only someone who watches a lot of TV like my aunt knows what it means to escape from an emotion.

One night Mia Farrow was on the show telling Conan about her sister Constance or Prudence, who seemed to be some sort of cross between a hippie and an elf. Anyway she was sent or taken or chaperoned to India at some point and upon being transferred to the third continent, she became a free spirit and met the Beatles and they all fell in love with her and wrote a song about her. She is now married somewhere in the Midwest and has a couple of children. Mia Farrow was not acting at all. She was just telling a story of her life in the guise of someone else, and it was just like an actor lying to herself. It was so natural. Conan interrupted Farrow many times but it didn't really matter; you couldn't really hear what he was saying because everything he said became something she was never going to say and so she could never really be interrupted at all.

Yet in spite of the Ho Hos and the interruptions of the unfunny at the Bear Park, I think and still think of the *Late Show* as a lovely program because it comes on so late and because it, unlike prime time, can afford to play back, ad nauseum, the dead invisible objects we repeat in our heads all day long. In this way, the show cancelled things before they happened. They cancelled my summers in Concrete, Washington. They cancelled my aunt's expectations. They eventually cancelled my aunt and my aunt's death, in the long years when I continued to watch late night television by myself. It is hard for me not to look at a television set today because somewhere in the world a TV set made my aunt disappear into the black and white wilderness that is the truth. This is something movies don't do because they generally try to make the nothings that don't exist into the nothings that do. But for me and my aunt, our days at the Bear Park comprise neither neurosis nor anxiety; they are merely an anecdote in retrospect, in the same way that scientists assure us that all the things we are thinking, the thing known as cognition, seeks its own sensations as if in a mirror—and so the mildest of hysterias is born when we gaze upon something we want to fall in love with. In the end, my aunt experienced many moods that she could not find for herself. I don't know why I watch TV so often and so lovingly and so mindlessly but I think it is because of my aunt. It is always something I am thinking that puts an end to something I am feeling. What is the end of something that is not funny? I think it is the cancellation of happiness. What is the love of things my aunt loved? I think it is another word, or maybe a desire neither my aunt nor I will have. A TV makes it almost impossible to reject the mood my aunt was having beside me.

One evening, as we are sitting in her office with the electric heaters and a metal box that holds the night's take sitting on her desk, my aunt turns, looks me in the eyes, and tells me that TV has taught her how to lie, and that westerns and Jackie Gleason skits, involving drunks and bad cooking in cramped kitchens, have helped her invent a new life and maintain her husband's old one (he barely participates in the hum drum details of a hotel, which he regards as a cartoon). Although my uncle never acknowledges the power of TV over his life, Jackie Gleason is the secret to the continual re-routing of my uncle's sleeping arrangements and his love (at least in my aunt's opinion) of my aunt and American politics, which, like my father's, centers around an unquestioned attraction to any person who happens to be deeply unpopular in our household at the moment. Such a feeling once directed itself to Richard Nixon (in the late seventies), and has recently addressed itself to Ronald Reagan. My uncle sleeps in room nineteen during the night, and my aunt sleeps in room twenty-two, on the second floor, during the day. I frequently hear Ronald Reagan's voice through the thin walls of the motel's rooms, the rooms in which my aunt and uncle never stop working. TV is probably what keeps the motel or maybe the mood of it running in the middle of other people's vacations, and it certainly arranges their family camping trips next to our late night TV shows. At any rate, Uncle Bing reads the papers voluminously. I don't know why I call him Bing or why my aunt is named Betty, but I think it has to do with Seattle and not Spokane, and the fact that the TV is never turned off at the Bear Park.

It is not easy to see what my aunt sees when she is sitting in front of the TV, but I think TV has made her understand that it is only by lying that someone can hold on to an emotion while simultaneously making a transition to another. Paul Newman called this general state of affairs the Kazan Transition and my aunt in her more optimistic moments called it a motel.[3] Of course, Robert Redford said of Newman that "the reason he's so demanding of himself is because he has no talent." My aunt has no talent for running a motel in the wilderness. She does not know how to boil an egg, make a bed, or even keep the books straight. For my aunt the wilderness isn't the woods or the deer flies or the brown bears that forage in her and Bing-bing's dumpsters but late night television, which my aunt loves and my uncle never watches because he thinks it is garbage.

Like most voices on TV, my aunt has two or three American voices, one separated by Mandarin, one by the so-called southern Chinese dialects, and one by an Amoy dialect (or Xiamen, as it is now called), all of which exist on the edge of some American version of melancholy.[4] The first voice is the English practiced by a Chinese person and

3 YouTube - Opry Mills Flooding May 3, 2010

... The largest hotel in the country outside Vegas, and you **called it a motel**. First of all, that "motel" existed in place with a theme park ...

www.youtube.com/watch?v=9QjnibGBf4c - Cached

4 The Edge of Melancholy: Shampoo

(11) According to the sleeve notes for the **Cinema** Club video version of the film , ... as it came to be known via the Group Theater and the work of **Elia Kazan**, ... dragged into the '70s: it was a **transition** that occurred later than ... along with Robert **Redford** and Paul Newman, whose careers and politics bear ...

archive.sensesofcinema.com/contents/05/37/shampoo.html - Cached - Similar

it sounds like an answering machine.[5] The second voice sounds like a Chinese restaurant in America. The third one, not always distinguisable to my ears, sounds vaguely American, or to be more precise, like a more colloquial voice from what I imagine is the southeastern part of China, what used to be known as the lower Yangtze Valley. Somewhat paradoxically, as my aunt has told me, it was in the *south*, in the lower Yangtze region that the *North China Daily News*, the newspaper of my aunt's childhood, was published, and it was there also that my aunt saw her first American movies and heard the singing of Fred Astaire and Ginger Rogers dubbed into voices singing Cantonese. All of this was, as any linguist can tell you, a good many years after the unification of the national languages in China, or rather, the instigation of a *kuo-yin* or national pronunciation that occurred in China in the 20s, before the years of the People's Republic. Together, these changes that had not quite happened when she was a child, along with the local and unlocal parts of my aunt's voice, make it hard for me to understand what my aunt was saying even though she was educated in (British) English-speaking schools in China and speaks English without grammatical mistakes. She speaks, in other words, a Chinese not spoken anywhere in China (anymore) and, now that she has been translated into a speaking region of the western United States, she speaks an American English not spoken by any other of the three hundred fifteen million or so speakers of English in America, except those speaking in the textbooks of language instruction printed in the U.K., or the audio tapes (*wai-kuo jen yung*—for use by foreigners) produced in China all through the 40s and 50s and designed for those westerners

---

5 I can still hear his **voice** - Simpler Living - Naomi Seldin ...

Feb 25, 2009 ... There are 16 messages on my cordless phone/**answering machine**. .... It **sounds like** you're honoring your father's memory in the right ways. ...

blog.timesunion.com/simplerliving/16-messages/6151/ - Cached who wanted to learn *p 'u-t'ung hua*, or the Beijing "national dialect." My aunt, who *already* knew Peking Mandarin as her second or third spoken language, used these audio-lingual learning tapes more or less backwards (though there is really no forwards way to learn a language one doesn't know), where the Chinese words preceded instead of followed the English ones on the tape. So while English speakers learned the Peking Dialect of Spoken Language Services, my aunt learned English Translation in Peking dialect. My recollection of my aunt's linguistic life, the only part of her that I *can* recollect, makes her appear as a type of linguistic biography that is not much written today but was prevalent during the nineteenth century, a biography where nothing is awestruck because nothing is hidden or concealed from view. In this sense, my aunt resembles the biography of a dead person where the dead person has somehow forgotten to die. She speaks casually, and the result of her speaking is also casual, and distant, like the speech of a language without a speaker. There is no original Chinese word for "motel," and no Chinese word for "concrete" either, and so my aunt pronounced the English words as if they *already* existed in Chinese, thus making out of them a concrete poem or a homophone from something in Washington state to something in a Wade Giles dictionary. In Chinese translation, *hun* means mixed, muddy; *nin* means to freeze, to congeal, to coagulate and *t'u* means earth, soil, and three mixed together make "concrete." And as for a motel, *ch'i* means steam or vapor, which when applied literally to a *ch'e* cart or barrow, becomes a motor car. This motor car, when driven to a hotel, stays a motor car but the building in front of it is a motel.

As any linguist can tell you, it is possible to read a thing without being able to speak it and it is possible to speak a thing without knowing what it is, and this is in fact how many people learn their second and third languages, which they suddenly hear, as if for the first time, when the meanings to words pronounced for hours in a classroom are delivered by a dictionary into an understanding. And this is how my aunt's understanding of her life in America was arrived at, as a delay in the speed of an understanding. In my aunt's case, this delay was a place called Concrete. In mine, it was an aunt. In other words, the proper study of an aunt is a delayed aunt, like a father who has passed away.

My aunt and uncle never had children of their own, but in the mid-80s they adopted a boy, Xaoshing, from Taiwan, who had been raised in an orphanage until the age of eleven and had been sent to a number of youth homes in Taipei. He was ten years older than me, and when I met him for the first time, he had just dropped out of high school. Like most of my relatives, who were not totally relatives but not totally non-relatives either, he became more like me as the age at which I remembered him passed mine, and I began, as I grew older, to write this down, more or less simultaneously. He stayed eleven in my mind; and all through my high school years and beyond, he was more than me, or more alive to me than I could be to myself. He was living with my aunt and uncle in Spokane. When we first went to visit, he did not come out of his room but only shouted something in a Chinese I did not understand through his door. On subsequent visits, when my mother had decided it would be best if I stayed at home with a baby sitter, he would come out of his room and sit in the living room where the adults were having tea, but refused to take part in the conversation. My mother later told me that there were a number of years when Xaoshing did not say a word to anyone in his household.

When he turned seventeen, the year before my aunt and uncle left Seattle, Xaoshing announced to his foster parents, in perfect English, that he no longer wanted to be their son. He asked for $500 and promptly flew back to Taiwan. He told my aunt and uncle that he wanted to be with his birth mother. He never wrote to his adoptive parents after leaving. Although my aunt and uncle never mentioned him, I believe they thought of him as their son, as they kept all his photos, his model airplanes, skateboard, basketballs and baseball gloves, stamp collection, all the things that were once his boyish American possessions, in a corner of my aunt's motel room, which was her living room and her bedroom. During the two years before her death, when my aunt was quite sick with pancreatic cancer, my mother sent urgent letters to Xaoshing asking him to phone or write his mother, but he never did. After my aunt died, Xaoshing returned to the United States, bringing his birth mother with him. I have tried to find Xaoshing on the internet and Facebook in the years after his mother died, with the hope of seeing the second part of his life somehow, but he has yet to turn up, and the various images that show up look either too old or too young to be the grown man he must now be. My mother refuses to speak of Xaoshing. She tells me that he is still angry with his family, and mine, for being a thing it was not supposed to be. For her, my aunt's death is inextricably linked to a middle-aged person who lives in America and whose last name she cannot know.

Unlike most twentieth-century biographies that labor under a naturalistic fallacy wherein the private life corroborates the life displayed in drugstore tabloids (a celebrity dies over and over again in the public's mind), my aunt's private life, the one that she lived with me in front of the Sylvania, is not really connected to anything private except the few TV programs that we watched and eventually forgot together, and so in a very real way my aunt, like my father who basically came after her, has never had the time to detach herself from me or her feelings, and being unable to do this, her death was extremely hard to explain. In the years since her death, I have come to see that my aunt does not bear any overt physical resemblance to the characters who appeared on programs we loved; there is no particular hair style or gait or exaggerated laugh that links her to something in particular, neither an adopted son nor an era of TV watching. When I turn on the TV, she is more like the person who is always already there, addressing the Biography Channel years before I had time to think about her life and death or cable TV. The uses of TV are just as ambiguous as the people watching it.

Most of our evenings at the Bear Park are spent in front of a TV watching late night television with a few cans of Pabst Blue Ribbon, and occasionally some Chivas Regal, which my aunt serves in Dixie cups from the bathroom or in restaurant Willoware tea cups. Our favorite shows, which are for me a kind of seasonal re-run of a preceding season, spring if I arrive in the summer, or winter if I arrive in the spring, are the late-night talk shows, especially the ones with guys like Craig Kilborn or Steve Colbert, who tend to wear nice suits and pretend to be telling the news and thus resemble news anchors who have not had enough to drink. This my aunt never really understands. She does not think anyone pretending to be straight or drunk can be funny.

One year, I'm not sure which, my insomniac aunt and I are deciphering black and white boxes of the stations in the *TV Guide*. We are stumped. The channels in the curved black squares don't correspond to the thirteen numbers on the TV dial. "The boxes are broken." My aunt adds, "like calligraphy."

Four, five and six are lucky rolls of the dice in China. I turn to channel five. My aunt says "eng," with a Cantonese accent, but the *Star Trek* re-runs are not on. We get MTV instead. My aunt nods. My aunt knows it's a taped kind of program.

"This looks good." I say.

"It's a re-run," my aunt says.

After a Pat Benatar song and a commercial with an astronaut saluting an MTV flag on it, followed by some beeping noises, they introduce someone who knows a special kind of shiatsu and he comes onto the set and starts practicing it live on Kennedy, who was MTV's *Alternative Nation* emcee all through the 90s. The shiatsu guy's English isn't very good and he is explaining patiently to Kennedy how I touch you and you touch me and everybody is touching everybody and no one can tell who is touching who if it's you or me and even though he isn't saying it well he is saying being touched isn't about touching someone else or being touched by someone else it is just about touching and more and more touching and about two people experiencing the same thing at the same time and whatever he is saying it is just a kind of touching. And Kennedy, who can be very funny, isn't being funny or sarcastic; she is embarrassed because she doesn't want to make fun of some Asian guy who doesn't speak English very well and because she doesn't like being touched by a stranger on TV and because it is sort of a joke but it is also a kind of enlightenment about touching and talking and who wants to be enlightened while watching MTV. The best re-run wouldn't even know that it was a re-run while it was being looked at.

All during this episode I am looking at my aunt looking at Kennedy. The drapes in the room are green. They resemble the feelings my aunt is having. And then they resemble the feelings Kennedy is having. And then they resemble the TV. After the episode, my aunt turns to me and says simply, "I like her." A minute later she adds: "You cannot see her eyes." I think my aunt is right. Deep down inside "that Kennedy person," as my aunt calls her, something is moving rapidly to the surface of my aunt's and my world, like those clips of guided missiles exiting

31

THE PAGODA
Elliott at Skyway
Paradise, Calif.

寶塔

ferociously from a body of water in the south Pacific. Of course, for my aunt and me the surface is a TV set and Kennedy is lying. The shiatsu guy doesn't know how to lie.[6]

After we finish watching, my aunt says she did not understand anything the shiatsu guy said. She asks me, "is the shiatsu guy drunk?"

I say, "I don't think so."

In the last letter I received from my aunt and which I have now lost, my aunt did not mention her son or the death of her husband two years earlier. The letter preceded my father's death by at least a year. In the letter, she confessed to me that it did not take any of her talent (she had been a chemist and physician in China) to run the motel at all and that that bit of luck was what had made her happy and that had given her a new life watching *Gilligan's Island* in the day and late-night talk shows at night. Like most things in my aunt's life, running a motel was a ritual enhanced by television. It was repetitive and beautiful. It was the opposite of metaphysical.[7] It was the geography of the living room in the discontinuous form of a TV broadcast. In retrospect, I now realize it was the re-run of something inessential in a life, or a death inside a life. The problem with most relatives is that they are never vulgar enough. The problem with a TV is you can never love it too

6 Manipulating Ethnic Tradition: The Funeral Ceremony, Tourism, and ...

by S Yamashita - 1994 - Cited by 12 - Related articles
FUNERAL CEREMONY, TOURISM, AND. TELEVISION AMONG THE TORAJA
OF SULAWESI ... based was made possible as a part of the research project on
"Cultural ...

www.jstor.org/stable/3351103

7 [DOC] The Terrorist and His Media (a rereading of - Module: MC412 ...

File Format: Microsoft Word - View as HTML
by G Steinberg - Related articles
However, when we get out of the idea of the mere redundancy of **ritual** and myth
.... society might be **made possible** because of the media (conceived as magic).
.... All those within reach of a **television** set are simultaneously and equally ...

www.democraciadireta.com.br/The_terrorist_and_his_media.doc - Similar much. Most of my aunt's and my conversations sounded like something on a TV. Nothing is more lonely than TV late at night with a relative you hardly know.

One evening my aunt was watching the TV a little carelessly as she liked to, and I was reading the *New Yorker* a little carelessly, too, and telling my aunt about Diana Trilling's account of her visit to the White House for a Nobel Prize dinner with the Kennedy's, in 1962, I think, the famous dinner when JFK said that this was the largest collection of creative individuals ever assembled in the White House except when Thomas Jefferson dined there alone. Diana Trilling, who performs like a vain and spoiled child in the piece, talks at theatrical length about the preparations of buying a dress, then another and then another without having to spend a lot of a poor intellectual's money (which she hoards repeatedly during the memoir), and the dress she first buys is too short and the wrong color—and one is not surprised. That and the Kennedy quote are about all I remember about the piece, and perhaps the men in military jackets who coach you and tell you what to do and the way JFK sits down very quickly and without regal pretensions. And how he exuded power. When I get to the dress part, my aunt interrupts. "I don't have a dress," then adds "Jackie's dresses are usually black or white." None of this matters now. Diana Trilling has died. So has Jackie. My aunt is gone. Ronald Reagan and my father's love for Ronald Reagan are dead too. One can hardly imagine that dinner and JFK's speech, but one does. These are the ways one has of feeling. If the world is white, then color is a form of redundancy. Diana Trilling's piece gives up. There are a few redundant colors in it but most of them are gone. TV makes me forget all the colors except the one with an aunt inside of it. An American TV station has many Chinese moods inside it just like we did, even if it is missing one or two of its actual family members. Once a mood like my aunt gets inside a TV set, it starts to die.

In the years before her death, I came to realize that watching TV with my aunt was a sort of autism in images before autism became a more commonly recognized diagnostic category and many years before it was understood that autism, like smoking or obesity, is amplified by the social circles it is embedded in. *Of course* autism produced a lot of people like my aunt. And then it produced a few of her multiple deaths. *Of course*, forgetting is among the most beautiful things that can happen to the human brain. *Of course*, the beautiful thing about a death is that it keeps multiplying. It is true that watching TV with my aunt, I experienced moods I could not find for myself, and those moods resembled a lover who has almost walked into a room or those patented colors produced by an expensive TV. As any mathematician can tell you, lovers like drapes are feeble signs of a light that can't come in, for the minute a TV show or a person becomes memorized (the worst form of recognition), it or she ceases to exist in any meaningful way. A dumb TV show is the most beautiful TV show. My aunt knew my love for her very well. She was clairvoyant and an insomniac. She knew that TV lovers are basically "undetectable, overwhelmingly numerous, unknown and unscientific. In short, they are hopeless."

part II

Yesterday night I was watching re-runs of Jon Stewart on Comedy Central, as he made fun of his guests, who were extremely beautiful (they were mostly models or rodeo queens) and who wore very nice clothes. Like Andy Warhol, Jon Stewart basically says the same thing to everyone. He tells them something like "hey you are looking good" and "hey you are wearing *really* nice clothes" and then he asks them "what is it? is that Marni or Marc Jacobs or Imitation of Christ?" and the guests start to look a bit embarrassed. Jon Stewart then says "hey where did you buy your clothes? I mean what store?" and "did you get them for free?" and what would he (Jon Stewart) have to do to get something like that for free because "my wife would probably look really nice in something like that." I particularly like to watch these segments twice when they are re-broadcast later on the same night on a different channel, which often happens in major metro areas. Anyway, such guests, whether they are sports stars such as Maria Sharapova, models like Tyra Banks, actors like Julia Stiles, or chefs like Nobu Matsushita are superior to other talk show guests (writers make the worst talk show guests) because everything they say is basically irrelevant to who they are, and because the guests are utterly unrelated to what they talk about, which makes them extremely fascinating from a somatic standpoint. A model from Belgium or a chef from Las Vegas, or a child from Kansas City who can imitate the sounds of strange animals like bush hogs or California condors defeats conversation before it starts—and this, of course, is what creates that beautiful thing known as talking. As my aunt knew, no one really hears you when you talk on TV. That is why it is easy to lie on TV, because it is just like real life.

Most of the talk my aunt and I do is posthumous by the time we're done talking. What my aunt didn't understand so well was that most relatives that we love are dead long before we get to them and that, probably because of the way she spoke her English, the best lies are the lies told by someone she didn't love to someone she did. That is why late night TV shows are often viewed in one's own bed with the lights turned low and the bedroom drapes pulled. Like photographs of photographs, such lies usually lead to depersonalization and anxiety. Yesterday after spending the night watching late night TV, I went the next day to see *Rushmore* by myself. I had a very good time. Last night, a model who resembled Amber Valetta said: "It would be useful to remember the middle names of each American president."

A few months after my aunt died, my mother sent me three gray Buster Brown shoe boxes containing the post cards my aunt had mailed her. Everything my aunt sent my mother occurred on half-filled in post cards, probably because they were the only form of communication that could be left unwritten in the space of a TV commercial and because stamps were cheaper than phone calls in the 70s and 80s. The frequency of the post cards, sometimes two or three times a week, gave them the appearance of being careless and un-letter like. Unlike phone calls or letters that were mailed from a foreign country and that arrived on the occasion of a birthday or anniversary like a gift, my aunt's postcards were more like half-private ads; they informed my mother, unpredictably and in sloppily written Chinese, of the day's weather in Concrete or a TV show my aunt was currently watching. The post cards were one of three photographic variations of a motel in Concrete or a single photograph of a Chinese restaurant in Spokane, which later was the same photograph of a different restaurant in Seattle. These postcards were the closest thing, in writing, minus the images of course, to a TV commercial. For my mother, these postcards seemed, although probably in retrospect, to allow too much of the present and too little history into them, largely because they were often based on *USA Today* weather reports my aunt had read for the part of Ohio my mother lived in, and because, in these post cards, my aunt would exhort my mother to take vitamins and Chinese herbal medicines in a week already past. For this reason, the post cards seemed to subtract from, and to add to, something from the present she was reading them in, and each post card invariably ended with a joke from late night TV that my aunt had transcribed to Chinese, with something untranslatable left out. The jokes were told in English but received in one of my aunt's southern Chinese dialects, which pretty much sums up my mother's relation to them. Like a dated weather report or most American things, they were plotless and not funny, and mostly incomprehensible to my mother, who grew up in Shanghai and who spoke a Xiamen dialect. When I asked her what my Chinese aunt had said in any particular post card, she would generally reply: "nag."

When I look at my aunt in these photographs, she and I appear in reverse chronological order. Yes, my aunt is only a Chinese photograph in a photograph that is not Chinese. She seems to be preparing footnotes for my death or preventing another one from taking place. Like a photograph, she is in love with the things of the world, one of whom happens to be me. For the last few years and under some unknown compulsion I associate with rock music on MTV, perhaps it is the compulsion to lie or not lie, I have removed most of the photographs of my aunt from the album, one or two at a time, as if some sort of "tell-tale compression"—not of the pages of a life, as in Jane Austen's *Northanger Abbey*—but of the images of a life were taking place. I think my aunt would have wanted to be removed from a family or a chronology in this way, for as with the numerous and unpredictable additions to a life, so too with its subtractions. As I've said earlier, autism produced a lot of people like my aunt. And then it produced a few of her multiple deaths. *Of course*, the beautiful thing about a death is that it keeps multiplying. The things in my aunt that I loved are things I couldn't make up or that don't appear at all. The only thing more boring and less anonymous than the Bear Park Motel or TV is probably watching too little of it.

It was not until after my aunt died that I realized that my mother listened to TV just like my aunt did. When I see them together, the one appearing to be a Chinese woman and the other appearing to be a non-Chinese one, they look like a Greek chorus watching *Oprah*, although they never actually did sit down and watch TV together. Nonetheless, watching TV with them made it possible for them to wait a very long time for something, I think it was my family, to arrive. And in retrospect, the family that arrived arrived somewhere outside my family, like a name on a postcard or a *TV Guide* laid on a green couch. Even after the programs they loved ended, their watching remained communal, vague, and nonsensical, like a premonition, or maybe like a half glass of milk sitting on the table. Watching TV with them was probably the best way to replace all the individual and deep feelings I have with something shallow and repetitive. Whenever I watch TV, many years later, I hear my aunt and the sit-coms and late night conversations that caused my aunt to ask the most unbearable questions, the invisible questions I associate with lies, the lies that *are*, in fact, a family or a TV being watched.

One late night at the Bear Park, my aunt turned to me slowly and without quite looking at me asked, "Are you in love with someone?" I was sixteen. I had not even kissed anyone.

I said, "Yes."

As I said, the future is imagined with far too few details. As I said, my aunt did not look me in the face when she asked the question.

People say you cannot imagine a thing like love coming from a TV set, but I think most of our family's feelings for each other started and ended there. After a good many years passed, as TV networks slowly migrated from sit coms to reality TV and the history of TV itself migrated to the internet, most of my aunt's moods ended up being replaced in my mind with the carefree numbers from a Hollywood musical. This could hardly be called a random form of identity formation, for my aunt always acted as if becoming American were a quantifiable chemical

operation that would make her rich. I am not quite sure of the economic foundation for this belief, but I believe it had something to do with locating the geographical coordinates of someone else's happiness or enhancing a family mood that tended to appear late at night when most accidents with large machinery are prone to happen.[8] Such a mood made a particular Asian family come alive like a commercial, and made them think about eating late at night.

When my mother moved out of her house in Ohio and into a retirement home in Pennsylvania, the years of my aunt's listening, unlike her talking, never did come back to me like the ghosts, poltergeists or other supernatural formations that sometimes inhabit a house. Even now when I think about it, somewhere a TV is watching over our family, and this action, an inaction really, is what makes TV, like a relative like my aunt, so minor, beautiful and post-colonial in its multiple transmission effects.[9] Because it is so boring, a TV, and here I am talking about any TV in the world, makes my aunt's feelings ambient and hallucinogenic in the moment I walk into the room. And now, like a bout of hysteria or a cold that has run its course, a few TV programs are all that I really have left of my aunt. She appears late at night, along with Sulu on *Star Trek* or the dying gazelles on the Mutual of Omaha's *Wild Kingdom*. She feels like the

8 WikiAnswers - **Footnote** to Youth Q&A - WikiAnswers Additional **Footnote** to Youth Questions [Page 2]. Footnote to youth tagalog. [Popularity 1] See question. What is **mood** of **footnote** for youth

...wiki.answers.com/Q/FAQMAP/6022 - Cached - Similar
Show more results from wiki.answers.com
just want to be a **footnote** in someone else's happiness

Mar 28, 2010 ... just want to be a **footnote** in someone else's happiness ... Current **Mood**: nostalgic. Leave a comment. emuhleex. 04 April 2010 @ 02:52 am ...

harlequingerhl.livejournal.com/ - Cached

9 **Retirement Homes**, Retirement Communities, Assisted Living & Senior ...

RetirementHomes.com is an online resource for **retirement homes**, retirement communities, ... Oregon, **Pennsylvania**, **Rhode Island**, South Carolina, South Dakota ...

www.**retirementhomes**.com/ - Cached - Similar

weakest of descriptions of things I can no longer see, a kind of half object or philosophical riddle dreamed up in China after the fall of the Kuomitang or Germany just after the wars. Now that they are dead, my aunt and father exist inside a place where the less-than-honest ravages of the world can finally be made to unfurl without the violence of the feelings that normally attaches to them. People like my aunt don't need to be remembered; they need to be forgotten inside a TV set. The era of forgetting isn't over, it just needs to be reinvented by databases.

Tonight many months have passed since I began writing all this down. Tonight, it is warm in southern California and I am getting stoned and thinking about T.S. Eliot and Mia Farrow and how, if it were really perfect, a writer's oeuvre like Constance's life and Mia Farrow's re-telling of it, everything the writer wrote, would automatically convert itself into a single long form where content is merely a form of creating noise, non-bliss, distraction, a troubled sensorium, bad planning, deprivations, or "the illusion of sociology," which is what happens on TV with shows like *Desperate Housewives*, shows that absorb as much unethical behavior from the environment around them.

My aunt has died and after she died my father died too. Tonight, my aunt's half-moods arrive in the room. They mirror the room and its furniture like a TV screen. They look like other people's clothing. I didn't fall in love with my aunt so I could fall in love with a made up thing; I made up things so that I could fall in love with her, continually and without end. In the room where I am sitting, something in the room, like a standstill, escapes from the four corners of the room or else gives off the illusion of being recorded. But love cannot record anything in a photograph or anywhere else. Sometimes you need a TV or a relative to do that.

My aunt understood all this perfectly, and accordingly her life feels longer and more boring than it

START FROM HOME

hollis summers

is, as if a strobe light were going off inside of it. Thus in the 90's, after my aunt had died and I was living in New York and going out and drinking a lot, my aunt's talking and non-talking slowly came to remind me of another culture, the Nuer, who live in northern Africa and regard all abnormal human births as hippopotamuses that are accidentally born to humans. In their minds the solution for such baby hippos is clear: "They gently lay them in the river where they belong." All the poems I gave to my aunt to read while we sat in the Bear Park watching TV have been dead for a very long time. I see them stand up and walk around the room. They look like animals that have been recently stuffed. They shed tears like pancakes. They move around like a little parade with felt-covered batons. They smell of department stores. They tell my father about used cars. They hand my mother grains of rice. They invent songs by Depeche Mode or Tears for Fears. And in this way I know that the things I am feeling are no longer exceptions to the things that recur.

My aunt and I liked the 80s too much. She passed away in 1987 one year before my father died, and I think that the source of my feelings is my aunt, who listened to me lie and who didn't understand what I was writing in the poems I gave her but liked them anyway. When I was in high school and college, I would give poems and stories to my mother and two professors who were my mother's colleagues in the English department at Ohio University: Hollis Summers and Wayne Dodd. I typed the poems out on a blue IBM Selectric that my father had bought for me from the Ohio University used equipment and requistions office. This became the typewriter that I wrote absolutely everything on in high school, eventually in college, and finally at Columbia in the 80s and 90s when I was working on my Ph.d. dissertation, whose many drafts I also typed on that machine. Because I was a fast typist and slow finisher, and because I was slow to buy a computer (I purchased my first computer, an Epson 8088 machine, with a nine-inch amber monitor, in 1988, in the months before my father's death), I produced innumerable paper drafts of whatever it was that I was writing through most of high school and beyond, and because I tended to work on many unfinished poems and dissertation chapters simultaneously, as soon as I had finished typing a poem, I would give it to my mother, or, if I were in Concrete, to my aunt, and both of them would usually stop whatever they were doing and read. And so in my mind there was no delay between remembering and not remembering or between my aunt living and my father dying in the pages that are to come, as if writing *now* were a kind of time-lapse photography. And I believe that this *now* can force brevity or the unacknowledged parts of tenderness to forget what time it was, forget those gentle colors on a shirt my aunt is wearing as she sits, smoking Camels in front of the TV or doing laundry in the middle of the night. As children instinctively know, and as all adults learn again when they fall in love, staring prevents a loved one from leaving. This has an unintended consequence: as one ages, it becomes harder to stare at a face unless one is staring at something one loves a little too much. But paradoxically, staring, especially later in life, removes most of one's feelings from the world and deposits them somewhere else, whether in childhood, a scrapbook, real life, a former girlfriend, a news story about ozone, a romantic French restaurant, a telephone call, or a movie. I didn't love someone like my aunt because of who she was, I loved her because she looked at me an awfully long time.

Today I remove the last of my aunt's photographs from this scrapbook. In this way, what you are reading no longer contains some of the things I have been telling you about. How can you describe an image anyway? I remove the picture of a woman wearing a white cowboy hat and throw it away. What does the thing known as a delay look like? I think it might be an image of a camera trying hopelessly to fall in love with a television or someone like my aunt. A TV or a photograph can teach a child to remember but none of these things can teach a child how to forget, and no child (up to a certain age) is very much upset by forgetting. Adults think a TV set can make the world go effortlessly away, if only for a half an hour, but children know that nothing mechanical, like the world or a TV set, is ever really remembered by those who are inside of it. The world my father and aunt knew and that I knew with them is just another word for a television set with a few of the world's colors removed. The things that we loved in someone else remain the things they always were long after he or she is gone, and they too go away. The phone rings. I let the machine pick up. I turn on the TV. I fall to sleep.

It is three p.m. and I am dozing off in the cab of a modified pick up truck on North Congress Street, in Concrete, Washington, opposite the court house and the jail, waiting for my aunt to come back. I am fifteen. I will turn sixteen in three days. Some of my memories are already dying.[10] We have driven into town to buy a few things: rubber bands for the shower curtains, Diet Coke, Mr. Clean, cigarettes, and Listerine. My aunt is wearing a Chinese-style shirt-dress that I will later learn the name for, and she walks hunched over to get to the only drug store, a Walgreen's, on Concrete's main drag. The town is mostly white and every time we come into the town center

10 The **Dying** Process - Signs the **Dying** Process has Begun

Nov 9, 2009 ... Often times these are people that have **already** died. Some may see this as the ... Barbara Karnes: Gone From **My** Sight: The **Dying** Experience ...

dying.about.com/od/thedyingprocess/a/process.htm - Cached - Similar

Dying at Grace (how much, hotel, home) - New Jersey (NJ) - City ...

They filmed several people though the process of **dying**. ... the whole show as it brought back so many painful **memories** of having to watch **my** .... as far as &quot ;playing God", my opinion is we **already** *are* when we ...

www.city-data.com › ... › US Forums › New Jersey - Cached - Similar

I notice a few people who stop what they are doing and stare at a Chinese woman who gets out of a Jeep Cherokee in the Pacific northwest and goes into a store to buy a pack of Camels or sometimes Virginia Slims and some Hostess Ho Hos for me. Occasionally, a few high school kids will stray past the cab and stare at me as if they are going to beat me up. I have often wondered why people stare at other people, in Athens, Ohio or in Concrete, Washington and it makes me think of the story my mother used to tell us about her and my father's first year in Seattle sometime in late 1956, after they got married. After getting back from a one-weekend honeymoon, my mother and father decided to rent a larger apartment together. They read the real estate ads in the local paper and then made phone calls in the morning. Many people from the neighborhood answered my parents' phone calls and they said things like yes, yes, it's a nice apartment, very clean, come over and have a look at it. But invariably, when my mother and father drove over to the house a few minutes later, and got out of their car, my mother in a Chinese dress and my father in a suit that was probably too big for him, a landlord would come to the door and say "I'm sorry but it's just been rented." Or many times, no one would even come to the door at all and my parents would ring it twice and then go home. And the only thing I really remember about this is that my father and mother never seemed angry when they told me this story, and that is probably one of the reasons I think my mother is much more beautiful than me and my father's anger is more blurry than that "litany of hate" that a scholar of Chinese-American history said was directed at the first few generations of Chinese people who came to America, and which was not rectified until the Civil Rights Act of 1964, when I was seven and my sister was five. As I sit in the cab and wait for my aunt, I hear the sounds of the street and an occasional horse, and then the sound of the street separates itself from the window of the cab I am sitting in,

just as a TV with its sound turned up too loud can make my aunt invisible on one of those late evenings at the Bear Park Motel. Of course, those evenings have not yet arrived. All the people who are watching the television know this. Of course, the end is still far away for my aunt and my father. Of course, the end comes before and then it comes after. Because what are the uses of pleasure if they cannot be repeated?

I want to leave with an image of the one thing that I had forgotten until a few moments ago because it is, like a book being read, a machine not unlike a photograph of a family. What the photo describes is a vending machine in the lobby of my aunt and uncle's motel, the machine from which she retrieved Ho Hos during our late nights in front of the TV. In the 70s and 80s when my aunt and uncle lived and worked in their motel, there were no convenience stores less than twenty miles away, and so all guests who stayed at the motel, including my aunt and uncle, relied on two vending machines to supply those things they had momentarily forgotten. In one of the vending machines, my aunt removed smokes from twenty-nine of thirty-two slots (she left Marlboros, Lucky Strikes and Virginia Slims) and replaced them with toothbrushes, combs, condoms, cheap underwear, Elmer's glue, Coppertone suntan lotion, band-aids, Bayer aspirin, Duco plastic cement, Dramamine, hair bands, bobby pins, Cracker Jacks, fishing tackle and hooks, Kleenex, Prell shampoo, Dial soap, Bic pens, a packet of used postage stamps, Ho Hos, a tiny squirt gun (for the kids), a Duncan yo-yo (also for the kids), Drum chewing tobacco, a twenty-four shot roll of Kodachrome, a thirty-six shot roll of Ektachrome, legal size envelopes, a can of warm Pabst Blue Ribbon beer (for some reason, my aunt thought it was illegal to serve cold beer from the soda machine but warm beer was OK), a mini Swingline stapler, rolls of coil stamps that she had gotten from the post office, and a few paperback novels left behind by guests, which my aunt stuck into any unfilled slot.

When I last visited in 1986, a year before my aunt died, I took a photo of the machine, and then bought a coverless version of Richard Brautigan's *Trout Fishing in America*, an anthology of contemporary American poetry edited by A. Poulin, Jr., and an anthology of science fiction stories edited by Issac Asimov, one whose cover showed a galaxy and a starship with a small image of an astronaut falling away from it.[11] I paid a quarter for each of the books. As you can see from the photo, this vending machine, a kind of jukebox curiosity cabinet, looks alive, like most memories do. And because it is silent, it reminds me of a family history, made up of a few visual reproductions and very little talk, as my father and aunt, who rarely spoke, quite plainly understood.

The vending machine may have been Concrete's only circulating library, a kind of general store or inventory of the life of a town that the town itself did not know it was compiling, and it may explain why my aunt and father were variable in their appearances and expressiveness, if they were *ever* expressive in their appearances. For my aunt, a vending machine was simply something she made of the line between convenience and inconvenience; it was a machine she put herself into and then departed from without much thought, or to put it more simply, it was an accommodation in the various lives that intersected so carelessly or blithely with it. But for me it was and still is an apparatus for the production of a soul, or at least a universal machine of observations in the world two people knew, each shaped like a flower or possibly the calculus of a brand name that perpetually adds and subtracts things from the world.

---

11 That is why I still prefer, to this day, reading anthologies rather than individual books. A poem like a person in an anthology has forgotten its author. Like a re-run or a flea market photo, it receives coaching from things next to it that probably don't like or can't understand it.

In the end, whatever that may or may not be, it was an observation that gives my aunt a posthumous life. Even now, the various brand names of computers and cameras compile the lies of a family or a world as if they were minor conveniences or intractable objects without which we cannot live inside ourselves, like the unarticulated flame of a bibliography or biography of the lives one family tried to have in America. From the outside, the vending machine looks like it doesn't belong where it does. But then suddenly it does, and then it mostly just looks like one of the versions of happiness I thought a family would have.

I would like to thank Clare Churchouse and Ahn for infinite patience and love.

Many many thanks also to Ethan Bumas, Patrick Durgin, Jonathan Flatley, Robert Hamburger and Gordon Tapper for reading and commenting on portions of this ms.

SELECTED BACKLIST:

HIEROGLYPHS OF THE INVERTED WORLD, BY ROB HALPERN

THE CHILEAN FLAG, BY ELVIRA HERNÁNDEZ, TRANSLATED BY ALEC SCHUMACHER

TÍTULO / TITLE, BY LEGNA RODRÍGUEZ IGLESIAS, TRANSLATED BY KATHERINE M. HEDEEN

STAGE FRIGHT: PLAYS FROM SAN FRANCISCO POETS THEATER, BY KEVIN KILLIAN

GATHERING, BY DEVIN KING

AMBIENT PARKING LOT, BY PAMELA LU

TOMATOES, BY NATHALIE QUINTANE, TRANSLATED BY MARTY HIATT

FESTIVALS OF PATIENCE: THE VERSE POEMS OF ARTHUR RIMBAUD, TRANSLATED BY BRIAN KIM STEFANS

HANNAH WEINER'S OPEN HOUSE, BY HANNAH WEINER, EDITED BY PATRICK DURGIN

KENNINGEDITIONS.COM